LOVE IS...

By Barbara Swaby

Illustrated by
Beverly Luedecke

*Printed on recycled paper,
to help preserve our environment.*

**LOVE IS...
CODE 91682**

TEXT ©1993 BARBARA SWABY

**ILLUSTRATIONS ©1993 CURRENT, INC.
COLORADO SPRINGS, CO 80941
PRINTED IN THE U.S.A.**

LIBRARY OF CONGRESS CATALOG CARD NUMBER 93-72093
ISBN 0-944943-60-8

Love is a rainbow.

Love is a smile.

Love is a butterfly on a woodpile.

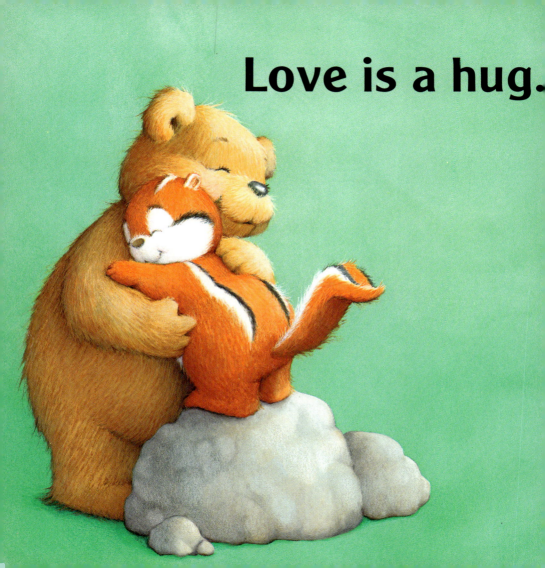

Love is a puppy curled up in a rug.

Love is a lollipop.

Love is a snowdrop on top of your nose.

Love is a blanket

Love can be most anything.